The Untold Tales of Yoziland

Mr. Tarky Finds a Purpose

Shivangi Nainwal

DEDICATION

To all of you, dear readers.

CONTENTS

CHAPTER ONE

*D*ear children, have you ever wanted to go to an enchanting world that abounds with splendid surprises at every corner? I know of two brave children who did go to such a land! Would you like to hear their story?

Then I must start from the very beginning.

It was the start of the summer holidays. Reyaan wandered around the house looking for something to do - or someone to pester. He found his sister Alisha perched on top of the bunk bed, reading a book.

"Come on, Alisha! Let's go out in the garden."

"Sure! I can read my book under the apple

tree."

"Certainly not, lazybones!" exclaimed Reyaan and dragged her out of the bed.

Once outside, Alisha threw a ball around for a while with Reyaan before plopping herself under the apple tree. Then she picked up her beloved book again.

Reyaan dropped next to her. "Come on now! You didn't play long enough! You are such a bookworm. What are you reading anyway?"

"It's a book where children go to distant lands and have many adventures," replied Alisha. "I wish we could go to a different place. We haven't been anywhere over the holidays!" she moaned.

"Ha! What if our very own apple tree were a portal to a different world?" said Reyaan, in jest. He shook the tiniest new twig growing from the bottom of the tree, "We could just shake this twig and tr…"

Even as he said the words, the world suddenly shook around them. The children felt a whirlwind engulf them and they were lifted straight off the ground!

"What's happening?" Alisha screamed.

All of a sudden, both of them fell back to the ground with a thud. But where were they? It seemed that they were still under their apple tree. But why did the place look so different? Where was their house?

"Reyaan, where are we?" asked Alisha in a daze.

"I don't know!" said Reyaan in panic. "I just shook this twig over here and…"

The very next moment, a whirlwind appeared again, and abruptly both the children found themselves back in their own yard.

"Whoa! We just beamed to a different place! Do you think that our apple tree really is a portal?" asked a very dazed but astonished Alisha.

"Looks like it is! And this little twig here seems to be the switch!" shouted Reyaan in excitement.

Now, the children were in a tizzy but not the least bit scared! "Let's try this portal again!" exclaimed Alisha.

But Mother was calling them inside for lunch. They finished their food without a squeak. The peas were polished off quickly, and the tower of rice was demolished in an instant. Mother was quite surprised and a bit suspicious at this sudden display of good behaviour.

As soon as they could, the kids were back in the garden to try out their newfound discovery. "Right, so how do we go back to the new world? Let's give the twig a good shake," said Reyaan.

Poof! Both the children found themselves in the strange place again!

"Wow, where do you think we are Reyaan? Is this another country?" asked Alisha.

"Maybe. Look, we have to be very careful here," said Reyaan, who was the older of the two and didn't want to get into any trouble.

Alisha looked up and saw that the sky was a deep purple instead of blue. "Wow, this is

surely another world, Reyaan! Look at the sky!"
she exclaimed, pointing her finger upwards.

But Reyaan was looking ahead. "We are in
someone else's garden, and there is a house
over there!" he said.

As he spoke, the door of the house opened,
and out walked a boy. He looked exactly like
the boys from back home. Only his clothes
were a bit different.

"Oh, hello! What are you doing in my
backyard?" Did you lose your way?" he asked,
a bit startled.

"Err.. no. Hello to you too! We come from
another world. Can you tell us where we are?"
asked Alisha.

"Another world! Really? That sounds amazing!
This place is Yoziland and my name is Bardek.
So, what superpowers do you have and how
did you reach here?" asked the boy, who now
looked awestruck.

The children quickly explained about the tree-
portal, the planet Earth, and about themselves.

Bardek was thrilled to meet someone from another world! He immediately wanted to show them his home.

So, Alisha and Reyaan sneaked into his room. It was strewn with clothes, books and a lot of other stuff.

"Just like back home!" exclaimed Alisha. She picked up a book. The cover looked interesting. "Do you like to read?" she asked.

"Yes, indeed," said Bardek. "I also like to eat," he said, pulling out a drawer from under his desk. It was full of candies. Bright, glittery ones! "Why don't you try some?"

Alisha and Reyaan did try some. The candies seemed far superior to the ones back home. Reyaan even pocketed some to eat later!

Soon enough, all the children were out on the street for a short tour of Yoziland.

The street looked deserted, but they spotted a man coming from the other side of the road. "Meet my uncle – Mr. Yapman," said Bardek.

Mr. Yapman was very friendly, and (*according to*

Alisha), he talked quite a bit. He went on and on about his sporting achievements and that one time when he grew the biggest vegetables. "You should have seen my cabbages. They are all gone now. Now, where did you say, you kids are from? I bet that you have never even dreamed of such big cabbages!"

"Indeed, we haven't," said Alisha politely.

"Kids, you must hear about my new hobby. I am getting pretty good at…" carried on Mr. Yapman.

"Err.. I think something in your bag is leaking," Bardek pointed to the bag that Mr. Yapman was carrying.

"Ooh, I must hurry back home! I will catch you guys later." The kids bade a very enthusiastic farewell and moved on.

"So how are you finding my world? Is it better than yours?" asked Bardek cheerfully.

Now wasn't he ecstatic that he had made friends with someone from another land?

"Well, some things are the same.

Unfortunately, we also have to eat cabbages back home," said Reyaan. "Why don't you show us your playground?"

"Sure, let's cut through this garden, follow me." Bardek jumped over the nearest fence.

As they ran through the lawn, Alisha spotted some beautiful flowers. "Hey, wait, stop!" she shouted. "I have to see these flowers. They look lovely!"

"Oh, we cannot stop here, or someone will catch us!" exclaimed Bardek.

As if on cue, the front door opened and an old lady stepped out. She looked quite cross.
"Why are you kids here? Are you selling something?"

"Err, no," stuttered Bardek. He looked terrified, much to the amusement of Alisha.

"Hello madam, do you want your garden tidied up? There are weeds everywhere," she said thinking quickly.

Now, our little Alisha is very smart! She expected a big "NO" from the old lady. That meant that they could be on their way to the playground.

Instead, the old lady brightened up immediately and said –
"YES! How many Fregets do you want for this job?"

"Frigats?" repeated Alisha, visibly confused.

"Ten, madam," said Bardek hurriedly while nudging Alisha.

"Very well then! The rake is over there. I am going out now but I will be back in thirty minutes. My garden better be neat by then!" she said. Then she locked the door and disappeared into the street.

"Alright, let's take off to the playground! We don't really have to do this," said Reyaan.

"WAIT! Ten Fregets is a lot of money and this will take only a few minutes!" shouted Bardek.

"Aha! Fregets is money. Sure, let's start cleaning the place then," sighed Alisha and picked up the rake.

As she haphazardly waved it about in an

attempt to clear some tall grass, she felt the rake hit something. "What was that?" she exclaimed when suddenly, an odd creature jumped out from nowhere!

"Look! A FOX!" shrieked a very alarmed Alisha.

"I am not a fox. I am a wamlit," said the creature.

"Eeeeeeeeeeeeek! The fox is talking!" shrieked Alisha even louder.

"Well, why not? I did go to school. We wamlits are intelligent AND hardworking."

"This is mad!" exclaimed a bewildered Reyaan.

"Well, what are you doing here?" asked Bardek, coming up behind them.

He seemed completely unfazed as if it were normal for animals to talk!

The wamlit came out into the open, walking upright on two legs! He did look a bit like a fox but was big. He seemed even taller than Reyaan. He had four ears instead of two. But the oddest thing about him was that he was wearing a shirt and carrying a box!

"I lost my job and home a few days ago. The old lady does not know that I am hiding in her garden. Please do not tell her!" he pleaded.

"Can you help me? Do you have any Fregets to spare?" he continued – a tad bit sad.

"Err.. not as yet. But if you can help us clean up this garden, we will indeed have some to spare," said Bardek.

"Oh, thank you!" said the wamlit gratefully.

Then he turned towards Reyaan and pointed to his back pocket, where a bit of candy was peeking out. "Say, good fella, can you also spare that sweet? I am kind of hungry."

"Oh…yes…of course!" replied a befuddled Reyaan, finally finding his speech back.

"Why can't you find another job?" he asked curiously.

"Alas, I am a wamlit, and it is difficult for me to get work easily. You see, humans want to work with other humans most of the time!" he sighed.

"Why is it so, Mr. wamlit?" asked Alisha.

"Oh, don't you worry about that little girl! And my name is Tarky," said the wamlit.

Bardek felt sorry for Mr. Tarky. "You should come back home with me, Mr. Tarky. I can hide you for a few days till you find work."

Mr. Tarky was very happy to take up the generous offer.

Soon, the garden was tidied-up, and more importantly for Bardek — the money was collected.

Then Reyaan and Alisha decided to go home as Mother could get worried. They told Mr. Tarky about their journey from the other world and promised him that they would come again the next day.

The children better rest well tonight! It will be a long day tomorrow!

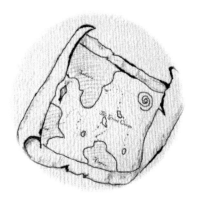

CHAPTER TWO

The next day, Alisha and Reyaan behaved very well. They took out the rubbish just as Father asked them to and even cleaned up their room. After that, they rushed back to Bardek's garden, but oh dear! Things did not look too good!

Bardek was outside his home, pacing worriedly. Mr. Tarky was nowhere to be seen!

"Where is Mr. Tarky? And why do you look like a dishrag?" asked Reyaan.

"I don't! Mr. Tarky has disappeared! He slept under the apple tree last night as I could not take him inside the house."

"Maybe he just left," said Alisha.

"He should have told…" started Bardek when suddenly there was a rustle among the bushes and Mr. Tarky appeared! He looked very buoyant.

"Oh, thank God! Where were you, Mr. Tarky?" asked Alisha.

"Oho, I just went for a walk to think about my future. I have thought enough! I will not look for another job!" he announced grandly.

"What? Well, then what are you going to do? I cannot keep you here forever!" howled Bardek.

"From now onwards, I will be a refordest!"

"A REFORDEST?" repeated Alisha incredulously. "What in the world is that?"

"Did you bump your head somewhere this morning?" added Reyaan.

"Kids, don't you have refordests in your world? A refordest looks for problems in the land, thinks of solutions, and then brings about changes for the good of everyone. The problems can be very big or very small! It does not matter."

"That sounds very noble, Mr. Tarky," said Alisha. She seemed very impressed.

"Bardek, I just need to spend a few days in your garden until I find another place to live," Mr. Tarky turned to Bardek.

"Of course, Mr. Tarky! You are welcome to stay here! No one will ever know," replied Bardek.

"Great! Do you want to be my assistant then? You can help me whenever you are free!"

"YESSSS!" cried Bardek with great animation. He was quite dazzled by the suggestion.

"Wow! That sounds marvellous! We also want to help you, Mr. Tarky!" exclaimed Reyaan.

"Wonderful! Now, will you chaps be kind enough and help me create a hiding place behind this apple tree?"

So, over the next few hours, the children gathered a lot of leaves and grass, and branches to help Mr. Tarky create a hiding spot in Bardek's garden.

After he was satisfied with his hideout, Mr. Tarky opened his box to take out his things.

Now, did he have anything interesting? Yes indeed! Alisha found a map of Yoziland among his things.

"Wow, Yoziland looks so very different from our world. Do you know that we have seven continents and so many oceans and seas! Does your world only have three?"

"There used to be five continents eons ago, Alisha. Now the seas have risen, and we are left with only three," explained Mr. Tarky.

"See? This is Salazia — where we live, this is Kramisk, and this is Alapas," he said, pointing towards the map.

"The two lost continents were here," he waved towards a vast ocean on the map.

"Oh, that is very sad. But I do love the skies in this world! The colour is such a lovely purple!"

"Lovely? Alisha, our skies used to be a

beautiful bright blue a long time ago. However, due to our greed, we polluted our environment and now the skies have changed to a nasty purple!" said Mr. Tarky.

"Polluted? But everything feels so clean here, Mr. Tarky. How is that possible? The air is better than our world and look at all the beautiful trees!"

"That is because we have covered Yoziland with a thin layer of Plitera. You cannot see it as it is very high up in the sky and covers the whole of Yoziland," said Mr. Tarky.

"Plitera? What is that?" asked Alisha.

"Our scientists developed Plitera to filter out all the noxious gases that we produce and release them outside into the space surrounding Yoziland," explained Mr. Tarky.

"It keeps this side of our atmosphere very clean, but as the gases and smoke now surround Yoziland beyond Plitera, our skies have turned purple. It makes me very sad," he sighed gloomily.

Mr. Tarky looked very dejected as he pondered

over the Yoziland skies but perked up the very next moment. "Say, you have given me a brilliant idea, Alisha! As I am a refordest now, my first job will be to turn the sky blue again!" he exclaimed.

"HA! Do you really think you can do it?" asked Bardek doubtfully.

You see dear readers, it is not exactly easy to turn the sky back to blue, right? How could Mr. Tarky pull this off?

"Of course, Bardek! Do you think I cannot manage this because I am a wamlit? Remember Bardek, there is a hidden flame inside each of us. Once it is lit, there is nothing that can stop us from achieving what we…"

"Oh great! Mr. Tarky is a philosopher too," muttered Bardek to himself. "How? You don't even have any Fregets!" he blurted out.

Reyaan jumped in excitedly. "I know what you should do! This happens a lot in our world. You should block the roads. Stop the traffic. Then someone will definitely listen to you. Won't cost a penny either…"

"What? No! We need to do something much grander. Something that actually helps us clean the skies!"

"Or, can we somehow punch a few holes in this Plitera of yours and bring it down? That will certainly wake a few people up!" chimed in Alisha.

"NOOOOOO!" shouted all the others together!

"Look kids, I have an old aunt and uncle who live on the other side of the river. They are very wise and always have some very good ideas. I think we should meet them."

"Well, I was hoping for some magical solution in this world. Isn't there some special diamond in a remote island that can cleanse this place? Or maybe some magic words that a mystic can tell us?" wondered Alisha.

Bardek laughed, "there is no magic here!"

"Well, you do have talking animals!" said Alisha looking at Mr. Tarky.

Mr. Tarky looked slightly offended. "What

does that even mean? Are you saying that humans are better than us?"

Reyaan shushed Alisha and said hurriedly, "okay then, let's all go! I just hope that we don't lose the way here!"

So, they all started on the other side of the river. It was a really long walk, and the children beheld many wondrous sights on the way.

On the streets, they saw several humans walking alongside many different creatures! And a number of these creatures were talking just like humans! It was very fascinating!

"Yes, Yoziland is a magical place indeed!" thought Alisha.

After plodding on for a very long time, they found themselves in front of a tiny hut. The hut looked very rundown.

Oh, dear! When was the last time it was painted?

"Why is the roof so low? How can anyone live in this hut, Mr. Tarky?" asked Reyaan.

"Oh, we wamlits mostly live under the ground. There are stairs right after the door. You will have to bend a little while getting in."

Mr. Tarky opened the door and disappeared. The rest followed.

They found themselves in an empty room that had a couple of tiny windows. There were some stairs in the corner leading under the ground.

The room below felt very cosy but seemed a bit shabby. The floor was scratched out, and paint was peeling from the walls.

"OH…HELLO….HELLO…   TARKY! HOW LOVELY TO SEE YOU! WHERE WERE YOU ALL THESE DAYS?" came a booming voice suddenly.

Alisha saw two wamlits in dressing gowns coming towards them with outstretched arms!

"Hello, uncle Huda and aunt Feyra! How are you? See, I have some friends who wish to meet you!" said Mr. Tarky, joyfully.

Bardek, Alisha, and Reyaan were duly

introduced. Uncle Huda and aunt Feyra were delighted to meet the children.

"Aunt Feyra! How are you?"

"Not so good," replied aunt Feyra. "But it's lovely to have some visitors at last! And that too from another land, you say! What a wonderful imagination your friends have, Tarky!"

"Aunt Feyra, they really are from another land!"

"If you say so dear!" said aunt Feyra, laughing heartily.

She quickly made hot chocolate for everyone and served up some delicious cake!

After tucking in the sweet treats, Mr. Tarky told uncle and aunt his reason for dropping by.

"Aunt Feyra... uncle Huda, we must do something soon! Where should we look first?" he exclaimed after explaining everything.

"I am very pleased that you are thinking for the greater good of the world, Tarky. But there is no simple solution for this. I will have to ponder over this for a while, and then we can talk again," replied aunt Feyra.

Mr. Tarky looked crestfallen. "Aunt Feyra, how long will we have to wait? What will I do till then?"

"Why don't you help me then, my dear Tarky? You are a refordest now," said uncle Huda.

"I would love to help you, uncle! Where should I start?"

"Our hut is getting very old, but we cannot afford a new home." Uncle Huda looked grim.

"And why is that?"

"The house prices have gone up like a rocket in the recent months! Do you know that burrows by the farming fields are twice the normal cost? And those by the water are four times! All this is because of the shoddy government policies!" grumbled uncle Huda. "Anyway, we need to make this home more liveable. A lot of work has to be done."

"Oh, that's terrible!" exclaimed Mr. Tarky.

"But recently, we have had so much trouble sleeping! Every night around midnight, we hear this strange hooting sound just like a sckowl," continued uncle Huda.

"It wakes us up every night! We have looked around everywhere, but haven't found anything. Not a sckowl in sight! It is very tiring in the day to go on with our work and get our hut fixed," added aunt Feyra.

"Can you stay with us one night and find out who is making this noise? We need to put a stop to this," said uncle Huda.

"Absolutely! And I will help you spruce up your house as well. Maybe one of you will have a solution for me soon."

Uncle Huda was pleased to hear that.

Now all the children also wanted to help. But they needed to sneak out in the night without the parents finding out.

It was decided that all the children would meet at Bardek's garden in the night after the parents fell asleep. Then all would triple-ride his bicycle to uncle Huda's hut.

Now, children, you should not get any ideas from this, okay? Sharing a bicycle ride is risky! Sneaking out when your parents are asleep is even riskier!

CHAPTER THREE

At nightfall, as per the plan — the children snuck out of the house! Reyaan had oiled the door hinges earlier, so they did not creak anymore, and Alisha had stuffed her backpack for the stakeout.

How fortunate they were that the Earth nights happened at the same time as the Yoziland nights!

Bardek was waiting for them with a strange-looking bicycle. It had a rider's seat and a long carriage box.

"Do you think that three people can go on

this?" Reyaan seemed a wee bit nervous.

"I have done this before with my friends! Hop on! Nothing can go wrong!"

Dear children, I am happy to report that the three kids made it safely to uncle Huda's home. They even enjoyed the ride – the little rascals!

Mr. Tarky was waiting at the door to greet all of them. Aunt Feyra had kindly laid a mattress in the garden. Since it was a lovely summer night, there was no need for blankets. It was quite dark though!

"Remember that the shrill sound comes around midnight. Be quiet around that time and keep your ears open!" cautioned aunt Feyra before heading back indoors.

Alisha gazed at the sky, as was her habit when lying outside. "Where are the stars, Mr. Tarky? Do you have moon and stars in this land?" asked Alisha.

"Yes, we do have a moon just like we have a sun. But unfortunately, we cannot see the sun, moon, or stars properly. Do you know why?"

"No."

"Because the layer of smoke outside Plitera is so thick!"

"That is so sad, Mr. Tarky!"

It was very sad indeed to live in a world where millions of stars in the universe could not be seen, and the moon was but a dull sphere in the night!

"Okay, now it is about to be midnight," whispered Mr. Tarky. "Everyone quiet! Whatever is making the noise mustn't hear us!"

They all stopped whispering and waited with bated breaths. It was very exciting for all the kids.

Well, at least before the shrill sound started.

"OOOOOOOOOOOOOOOOT! OOOOOOOOOOOOOOT!"

Alisha jumped under her skin. She was terrified!

In truth, everyone was terrified, including Mr. Tarky!

But he had to put up a brave front, didn't he?

"You kids stay here − I will go and check."
"OOOOOOOOOOOOOOT!" The shrill sound came again, but there was no one to be seen! Mr. Tarky ran up and down and sideways, and all around the house but he could not see a thing!

"Whaaaaaaaaa!" Alisha could not stop herself from screaming.

"Don't scream," whispered Reyaan, and then almost immediately, he jumped up high in the air!

Now, why was that, dear children? That is because the next "OOOOOOOOOOOT" came directly in his ear!

"Owwwwwwwwwww!" he yelled in pain.

"What's happening? Is it a ghost?" A very shaken Bardek switched on the flashlight that he was carrying.

And then he saw something tiny. A very tiny creature sitting on Reyaan's head.

"There's a bug in your hair!"

Reyaan shook his head while jumping about, when   suddenly......
"OOOOOOOOOOOOOT!" the tiny creature blasted out!

My, my! What a powerful voice for a creature so tiny!

"This is the one!" Reyaan screamed and managed to trap the creature under his jumper before it got a chance to disappear!

Mr. Tarky came running from beyond the garden. "What happened?" he gasped.

"We caught it, Mr. Tarky! It is a tiny creature! Makes such a loud noise though. You would think it is a woff or something!" said Bardek, brimming with excitement.

"Well done kids! Let's take it inside!" said Mr. Tarky.

Then he carefully picked up the jumper with the creature still howling quite loudly!

"What happened, did you find it?" Uncle Huda and aunt Feyra jumped up to their feet.

"Yes, we did!" yelled all the kids.

"It is under this jumper. We have to be a bit careful. It may sting or bite us or try to escape," said Mr. Tarky.

"I have never seen anything like this!" declared Bardek.

Mr. Tarky kept the jumper on the table, and everyone crowded around it. The howling had stopped.

"Gee, I hope that it is not dead!" said Alisha.

"Let me out of here!" Abruptly, a piercing voice came from underneath the jumper.

Everyone was astonished.

Well, to be very frank, dear children, I was quite astounded too! I did not expect a bug to be giving orders like that!

Mr. Tarky quickly shook the jumper and out leapt a stunning creature! Now that it was on the table, it did not seem like a bug at all! Instead, it looked like a very tiny teddy bear! It was very shiny too! All golden!

"Who are you? gasped Mr. Tarky, in utter bewilderment. "And why are you scaring my aunt and uncle?"

"Aah, so much better now. Can I get something to eat?" said the creature as it shook and arranged itself comfortably on the table.

Everyone just stared wide-eyed at it, too awestruck to reply immediately!

"Well, I suppose that was a bit rude of me. Hello, I am an Anista and I travelled from a faraway land. I am very hungry!" it said.

"An Anista?" exclaimed Mr. Tarky.

"Oho, an ANISTA!" uttered aunt Feyra loudly. "I was wondering why you look oddly familiar! But I thought that Anistas had gone extinct years ago? How did you get here?" Aunt Feyra had many questions.

"I saw you fly! Where are your wings?" Alisha had even more questions!

"Wings, what wings? I am not a bird! I can just fly using my arms. Look!"

Dear readers, I was as enthralled as everyone else in the room when I saw that, this little creature could fly simply by waving about her arms!

She flitted around the room and back to the table again.

Uncle Huda was shaking his head in disbelief. "You ARE an Anista! No other creature flies like this! Are there more of you? You shouldn't be here!"

"Yes, there are more of us. We didn't go extinct. We just hid when humans started catching us for our shiny skin. They used to put us in glass jars where they could see us flitting about."

"These humans..." mumbled Mr. Tarky to himself.

The children looked a little bit ashamed, and Mr. Tarky caught himself.

"What should we call you?" asked Bardek.

"I am Ruby," said the Anista.

Ruby continued with her story. "I got very

bored of hiding all the time and decided to see the world for myself. I stole out of our hiding place one night and left my family."

"I flew to so many places and had many adventures on the way. But now I want to go back home, and I do not remember the way!"

"Well, miss Ruby, why do you howl in front of our house every night? Someone could have caught you!" asked a puzzled uncle Huda.

"I am too tiny to get caught, and no one expects me to be here! You see, every day I get hungry, but I have nothing to eat! So, every night when I howl by your window, you open it to see who is making the noise. Then I simply hop inside and eat some of your leftover food!"

"I have done this in many other places. This trick has always worked, but I cannot do this forever. I need help to get back home."

"When I saw these little kids today, I thought that they might help me. They did not look cruel," she continued.

Yes, they are very nice kids, I assure you, dear readers. Only —

Reyaan is sometimes unkind to Alisha. And Alisha can be a bit annoying to Reyaan. Like the last time, she stole his… but I digress. On with the story, as all of you are getting impatient, I can see.

"We will help you get back home to your family, Ruby! Where do you live?" asked Alisha.

"Alas, Anistas used to live in the other continent - Alapas. You kids cannot help her get there. None of us can. It is very far," said uncle Huda.

"I think that I will have to hand you over to the local police station, where they will help you get home," said Mr. Tarky.

"NOOOOOOOOOO!" shrieked Ruby.

"My, my! How loud you are, despite being so tiny!" exclaimed aunt Feyra covering her ears.

"No one else can know that we Anistas are still alive! We will be caught again or even killed! And all because of me!" screamed Ruby in agitation.

"Do not be afraid, Ruby! Not all humans are

wicked these days! Some of us do care about the world. We can do so much more for you if everyone knows of your existence! You will not have to hide forever either!" said Bardek in an attempt to calm her down.

"Hmm… are you sure that no one will hunt us for our shiny skin? I cannot even bear to think of it!" Ruby shivered.

"You have every right to live in this world as everyone else! Look, why don't we take you around our town and then you can see how friendly our world is now? Everyone has a place under the sun," said uncle Huda.

"At least that's what they say," mumbled Mr. Tarky under his breath, yet again.

Oh dear, our Mr. Tarky is quite a mutterer, isn't he?

"I will show Ruby the town tomorrow. You should stay at home and rest well!" he said to uncle Huda.

"And we will join you! But for now, I think we should get back, as this case is solved!" declared Bardek.

So, all the children went back to their respective homes, and finally, uncle Huda had a good night's sleep! Aunt Feyra, however, was still wide awake, because you see, uncle Huda snores quite loudly!

CHAPTER FOUR

The following morning, the kids woke up late, much to the surprise of Mother and Father.

"Kids! You are out playing the whole day! No wonder you are unable to wake up on time! And when do you plan to pick up your school books? You have not studied a word during the summer holidays," chided Father as he served up some pancakes for breakfast.

"You will help me clean the kitchen cupboards in the morning, and then you will study in the afternoon. No outdoor games today," announced Mother.

"But MOM!" both kids shouted in unison.

But Mother listened to none of their excuses. The entire morning was spent rearranging the spice-racks and the afternoon was spent gazing at some numbers.

"What a waste of a day! I was so looking forward to hopping around Yoziland with Ruby!" exclaimed Alisha when finally, they were allowed to play.

"And Bardek and Mr. Tarky!" added a glum Reyaan.

"Let's behave well today so that we can go tomorrow. Mom is coming. Look at your books now!"

So dear children, one entire day was 'wasted' according to the kids. I wonder what happened during that day!

The next day when the kids reached Bardek's garden, they could not see him anywhere.

The kids wondered what to do next and decided to roam around the town to see more of Yoziland. Maybe they would bump into others somewhere.

As they ambled around taking in all the wonders of Yoziland, they ran into Bardek. He looked rather frantic and sweaty!

"Oh, there you are!" he shouted, spotting the children. "Where were you yesterday? We were waiting for you. But quick! There is no time to talk! We must hurry!"

"Hurry? Hurry for what?" asked Alisha, taken aback by Bardek's urgency.

"We have lost Ruby! She disappeared last afternoon while we were roaming in the town centre! Mr. Tarky is looking for her on the other side of the town."

"WHAT? exclaimed Reyaan. "How could you lose her? But, let's not worry too much. The last time, when you lost Mr. Tarky, he turned up on his own. Just wait – she will also show up somewhere."

"No, we cannot be sure. We MUST find her soon! No one else should find her before we do!" declared Bardek.

The anxious kids started running towards the town centre.

"How did you lose her? Where did you last see her?" gasped an out-of-breath Alisha.

Bardek went on about it in great detail, but I will tell you the whole story in fewer words.

Mr. Tarky and Bardek took Ruby to the local market. Ruby was safely hidden in Mr. Tarky's front shirt pocket so that she could see everything easily without being spotted. She got rather excited seeing so many shops after such a long time.

Bardek spent most of his Fregets buying her loads of snacks – cake, cookies, ice cream, and crisps.

Then they all went to a candy shop as she had never seen one before. There were so many candies on display that even Mr. Tarky got distracted. And within seconds, Ruby had disappeared!

Poor Mr. Tarky and Bardek searched high-and-low for her in the shop but without any success. They could not ask the storekeeper for help, as they had to keep Ruby's secret safe.

"We have looked everywhere! Mr. Tarky has also checked the area around uncle Huda's house! But she is nowhere to be found!" wailed Bardek.

They all reached the town centre and found Mr. Tarky wandering around confusedly.

"Oh, kids! How we missed you yesterday! We have lost our dear Ruby!" he howled.

"Don't worry, Mr. Tarky, we will help you find her. Should we look around in the candy shop again?" asked Reyaan.

"She is not there. I have already gone there twice. The shop owner is giving me queer looks now."

"How did we find Ruby in uncle Huda's house?" wondered Alisha aloud.

"You screamed, and then Ruby saw you. She said that she liked kids as they don't scare her," said Bardek.

"Maybe she got lost and hid in some other kid's

pocket? Is it possible? There must be so many children in the candy shop," said Reyaan.

"It is possible! There was only one kid in the shop when we went in yesterday. And I know him! His name is Pintu," said Bardek excitedly.

"Why would Ruby go with your friend when she was safe with us?" said Mr. Tarky, despondently. He looked very miserable.

"But we can still try. Let's go to Pintu's house and snoop around," said Bardek, feeling hopeful.

So, off they went to Pintu's house, which thankfully was not very far.

Bardek went inside the house to talk to him and look for Ruby.

He had to use all his skills to tour Pintu's entire home without raising any suspicion! However, he could not find her anywhere.

The others sneaked into the garden calling out for Ruby in hushed whispers.

"Ruuuuuuubbbbbbbbyyyyyyyy……….."

whispered Alisha many times.

"Shhhh… Alisha, I think I can hear something," said Reyaan.

They all stopped and listened intently. And then they all heard a very faint "Oooooooooot".

"Ruby, where are you?" whispered a very excited Alisha.

"Over here," came a faint voice.

It was Ruby! But where was she? And why didn't she reveal herself?

Mr. Tarky and Reyaan looked carefully in the bushes while Alisha scanned the flowerbeds. She finally found her, hiding under a flower!

Oh no! Something was wrong with Ruby! She looked very weary and scruffy.

However, she cheered up instantly on spotting Alisha. "You came to find me!" she squealed joyfully.

Mr. Tarky and Reyaan came running towards

the flowerbeds.

"Oh, my dear Ruby! What happened to you? Why did you run away?" Mr. Tarky shouted out aloud, forgetting that he had trespassed into someone else's property!

"Shhhh… let's all get out first," whispered Reyaan.

Mr. Tarky picked Ruby carefully in his palm as she was wincing with pain. "Don't worry, Ruby, we will fix you but let's first wait for Bardek," he said.

Bardek was very relieved when he got out and saw Ruby!

Then they all headed back to uncle Huda's house while Ruby narrated her story.

At the candy shop, she found the sights of a million colourful candies so exhilarating that she could not stop herself from flying out of Mr. Tarky's pocket!

She dived into one of the candy bins to taste some of the delightful confections when suddenly someone scooped her up along with the sweets!

Then she found herself being shoved into a packet along with all the candy.

We all know that it was Pintu who had bought the sweets!

Now, Ruby was rather scared and did not want to be spotted, so she kept very still till Pintu reached home.

Pintu would have discovered Ruby easily, but fortunately for her, his mom insisted he finish his lunch first.

The moment Pintu went out of the room, she wormed her way out of the packet, and flew out through the open window.

Unfortunately, in her hurry to escape, she smacked right onto a tree in the garden and sprained her left arm.

As she could not fly till her arm healed, she spent the night in the garden – lamenting over the loss of her newfound friends.

"I was soooooo afraid of losing all of you forever! And now I am very glad that I found you again," declared Ruby on reaching uncle Huda's house.

"We are also very happy because you are alive and well!" said Bardek.

"But Ruby, I don't want to lose you again. I think you should go to the police after you have healed. They will send you back home safely," said Mr. Tarky.

He was almost sniffing when he said that.

Poor Mr. Tarky!

"But Mr. Tarky, I do not want to go home just as yet!" exclaimed Ruby.

"Really? Why? Don't you miss your family anymore?" asked uncle Huda.

"All of you have shown to me that the world has changed a lot, Mr. Huda! You have been so kind to me!"

She continued "I think I want to spend some more time here before going back home. I want to see more of this magnificent world with my wonderful new friends!"

"But where will you stay till then?" asked Alisha.

"Can I stay with you for a while? I like all of you very much. I would try to behave myself and not be so greedy again!" Ruby asked aunt Feyra.

"Of course! That would be lovely!" exclaimed aunt Feyra as she tended to Ruby's injured arm.

Mr. Tarky was delighted too! "You can help me as well, Ruby! Do you know that I am a refordest?"

He then turned to uncle Huda, "And that reminds me, uncle! Do you have any solution for our purple skies?"

"We are still thinking about it. Why don't you stay a few more days with us, Tarky? You can also help me mend my roof. You know that my back hurts a bit," said uncle Huda.

"Yes! And we can all discuss any bright ideas as well!" added aunt Feyra.

"That will be fabulous!" exclaimed Mr. Tarky.

So, it ended well for dear old Ruby and even better for Mr. Tarky! You see, he wouldn't have to sleep in Bardek's furniture-less garden!

CHAPTER FIVE

*D*ear readers! Now we have our band of five adventurers! Mr. Tarky — the leader, Bardek, Alisha, Reyaan, and Ruby! Do you think they can turn the Yoziland skies back to blue? I think it might be a tad bit difficult, but let's see what happens next!

The next few days were busy for Mr. Tarky. He repaired the roof of uncle Huda's hut and painted all the walls. He even fixed a leaky pipe inside so the walls were not damp anymore.

Little Ruby also pitched in after her arm healed and ferried around various tools in her tiny hands.

For her tiny size, Ruby was quite sturdy indeed! Then one day, uncle Huda declared, "You are such a wonderful nephew, my dear Tarky!"

"While you were working so hard, aunt Feyra and I met a few of our old friends. Guess what? You may be a bit closer to the solution!"

"Hip…hip….hooray!" shouted Ruby from the corner.

"Really, uncle? Quick! Do tell us more!" exclaimed Mr. Tarky.

"One of my friends has told me about Mr. Patra, who is an eminent scientist in the wamlit community! He even has a science lab in his home! He may be able to help you. I can send a letter of introduction if you go to his house to meet him. You can borrow my car!"

"That sounds perfect! I will also ask others if they would like to join me on this trip!"

What do you think, Mr. Tarky? Of course, they would!

And so, in the next few days, all five set out excitedly in uncle Huda's car. Mr. Tarky drove all the way and did not stop until he reached

Mr. Patra's house!

Ruby decided to hide under Alisha's hat before Mr. Tarky rang the doorbell.

Mr. Patra seemed to be a very cheerful man. He lived alone and had all sorts of bizarre contraptions in his home!

I would have told you about those, but alas, I will be talking about it the whole day if I start!

He was delighted to hear about Mr. Tarky's quest!

"I hear you, Tarky. I am so glad that you brought this up. Some years ago, I was working on this idea of cleaning up the pollution outside Plitera, but I gave up because none of my ideas worked," he said.

He turned towards the children, "Kids do you know what is polluting the air?"

"Ummmm…. I do not…" mumbled Alisha hesitantly, but Bardek spoke at the same time, quite loudly.

"Of course! We all know that it is

ZIRIODIOXIDE!"

"Correct! Ziriodioxide forms from the element Zirio, which is the main pollutant in Yoziland."

"First, we need to find a way to suck it out from the atmosphere beyond Plitera. Then we need to change our ways so we that we don't pollute our skies as much."

"I have a machine in my garage, which is currently not working. It is supposed to fly and run around in circles outside the Plitera. If it works correctly, it will absorb the harmful gas – Ziriodioxide and split it back into Zirio and Oxygen."

"Why doesn't it work, Mr. Patra?" asked Bardek.

"I need a special substance for the process to work. I tried all the possible combinations but could not find the perfect stuff!" replied Mr. Patra.

He paused for a moment to think and then continued. "Well, actually to tell you the truth, children, the machine has worked, but only once. Now I would have told you a secret, but then you will call me a MAD scientist!"

"No... no... you must tell us! We are very good at keeping secrets!" said Reyaan excitedly.

"Okay then, but come closer, all of you," Mr. Patra suddenly dropped his voice and started whispering, as if someone else would hear him.

Everyone gathered around him.

"I had a human colleague known as Professor Hedra, who was very smart. You may have heard of him, Tarky. He knew that I was working on a machine to clean up our atmosphere."

"One day, he came to my home claiming that he had found the solution for the polluted air of Yoziland. However, he wanted to test it in secret, in my lab first."

Mr. Patra continued that Prof. Hedra brought a new substance for the test. "Hedra claimed that it was not from Yoziland."

"I thought that this new substance was brought into Yoziland by some crashing asteroid. But no, Hedra said that he had found a portal to another world!" said Mr. Patra.

"Can you believe this UTTER NONSENSE? NEITHER COULD I! However, Hedra insisted that he could travel to another world! And in this other world, this substance is known as Potassium."

"Potassium!" exclaimed Reyaan. "Was he talking about Earth?"

Mr. Patra looked astonished! He could not speak for a few seconds. "That is what Hedra said! How do you know about planet Earth?"

"We will tell you, Mr. Patra, but this time YOU have to keep our secret!" yelled Alisha, jumping up and down!

And so, it was time to tell Mr. Patra everything right from the beginning. Even Ruby jumped out of Alisha's hat to give another shock to Mr. Patra!

"Dollicking daylights! This has been some day!" exclaimed Mr. Patra, who was completely overwhelmed by the revelations.

"We used the bit of potassium that Hedra brought with him, and surprisingly, my machine did work! But I never believed Hedra about the other world, and he left in a huff."

"He disappeared a few days after our conversation, so I presumed that he simply stopped talking to me!"

"Now kids, you tell me that this other world — 'Earth' actually exists! Do you think Hedra is currently on planet Earth? He was saying something about getting more potassium before he left!" said Mr. Patra.

"Mr. Patra, we can go back to Earth and get you more potassium!" exclaimed Alisha.

"No! You are little kids. You cannot just go and play around with stuff! It can be perilous! We need an adult for this mission. Tarky, can you go to their world?"

Now Mr. Patra would have gone himself, but he had many other things to do!

"Of course! I will simply blend with the other wamlits on planet Earth — just as Reyaan and Alisha mingled with the humans here!"

"What? No! There are no wamlits on Earth! People over there have never seen talking animals!" said Reyaan.

"They might even put you in the zoo!" shrieked Alisha.

"What's a zoo?" asked Mr. Tarky.

"Ohhhhhh! Then what are we to do?" exclaimed Mr. Patra.

"I think we can dress up Mr. Tarky as a human being," Ruby piped up. "All he has to do is to buy potassium from a shop. We will need some Fregets, though," she continued.

"You can't just go to a shop and buy potassium!" chorused Reyaan and Mr. Patra.

Mr. Patra thought for a minute before asking Reyaan, "Do you think that you can find Hedra instead? He may be in your world."

Reyaan shook his head. "Earth is huge, Mr. Patra. He can be anywhere. When did you last see him?"

"It was almost a year ago. But you said that the

portal leads directly to your garden. What if he is somewhere in your town?"

"Even then, how will we find him? And he left such a long time ago!"

"We should at least try, Reyaan! What if we do find him?" interrupted Alisha.

"Alisha is right! Kids, I have his photo somewhere. You have a good look at it and try your best. If you are unsuccessful, we will think of something else," said Mr. Patra.

"And remember that I am coming with you. This is my mission after all!" said Mr. Tarky.

"We will also join you!" said Ruby and Bardek together.

Mr. Patra looked very pleased with the turn of events!

Immediately, plans were made on how to hide Mr. Tarky and Ruby. There were talks of creating a hideout in the garden. Bardek would come and go during the day, just like Alisha and Reyaan.

Mr. Tarky took the photo from Mr. Patra, and everyone headed for planet Earth!

OUR WORLD kids!

♠

Now I must say that Ruby, Bardek, and Mr. Tarky were completely fascinated by the sights of our world. They had never seen such beautiful blue skies before.

Bardek wanted to traipse around the town first, but a big task lay ahead of him, so he got to work instead!

Fortunately, the children's garden had a lot of bushes that they used to create a den for Mr. Tarky and Ruby.

Reyaan got his spare bedding and a torchlight for Mr. Tarky. Alisha snuck out her dad's old coat, glasses, boots, and a hat from the storage.

Thank God that it was summertime, so dad wouldn't miss any of these. Mr. Tarky wouldn't say the same though, as it was too hot for him to wear a coat in summers!

"This coat is too long for me, and everyone will

think I am a fool! I should have worn my own clothes!" he complained.

"But your clothes are a bit out-of-date. Besides, this hides you very well! Let's try your new look on a few people, Mr. Tarky!" suggested Bardek when he was satisfied with the disguise.

So off they went — all five of them, to the streets.

Bardek was very surprised to find only humans on the roads. "There are people everywhere! Where are the rest of the creatures? It is so strange," he said.

"Forget about strange. I hope no one will laugh at me!" said Mr. Tarky. He looked very uncomfortable indeed!

But no one laughed at him. People were too polite. "Rather chilly today for a summer's day, isn't it?" shouted one passerby to Mr. Tarky.

Well! Looks like everything went well for Mr. Tarky! No one recognised his disguise except for the neighbour's dog, who kept yipping at his boots! Now, Mr. Tarky was very glad that Earth-dogs don't talk!

CHAPTER SIX

Alisha woke up early in great excitement the next day. "Where should we go first? How can we ask about Prof. Hedra? Should we put up some 'Missing Person' posters around the street?" she had so many questions for Reyaan.

"No! That will not work," said Reyaan. "I think we should ask mom first. She will tell us what to do."

So, at the breakfast table, Reyaan tried to sound very nonchalant.

"Mom, if we have to find a missing person, where do you think we should start?"

Now, Mother was used to Reyaan asking silly questions all the time.

"Hmm… I think you should go to the police."

"But if we don't want to go to the police?"

"Then you should go to the newspapers." Mother played along.

"Thanks, mom!" Reyaan thought that was a lovely idea.

Later, Alisha took some breakfast leftovers for Mr. Tarky and Ruby. Some brainstorming was done over the cake crumbs!

"Let's put a message directly for Prof. Hedra in the papers. He can reply to us when he sees it!" said Alisha.

"But, how will he reply?" asked Mr. Tarky.

"He can send a letter to our house!" replied Alisha.

"Yes! We will keep a close eye on the mailbox," added Reyaan.

The kids didn't want the parents to discover their not-so-little secret!

Now, the plan also required some money, so the children broke their piggy banks and counted what they had.

They were really generous kids, weren't they?

"I think I should go to the newspaper office. I am old enough, and I don't have to pretend to be a human!" said Reyaan.

"Hmm. The paper may not take you seriously, Reyaan, as you are still a child. Let me speak at the office. I will try my best to look like a human. You can come with me, in case there are any problems," said Mr. Tarky.

Of course, others did not want to be left behind, so off went all of them – to the newspaper office. Ruby hid under Alisha's hat again.

A friendly receptionist greeted them, who said, "Hello! I am Mary, do you have an appointment, Mr…"

"Tarky!" said Mr. Tarky. He extended his paw

but then swiftly withdrew it.

"Alas! I do not have an appointment, Miss Mary. Our uncle has suddenly gone missing. We want to put an advertisement for him."

Mary looked at Mr. Tarky with some interest. He looked very peculiar indeed. Almost like a gangster!

"Missing person? Have you reported to the police?"

"Err… no. You see, my uncle is a bit eccentric. He may just be hiding somewhere. Here look at this photo. We only want to send a message to him through your paper. How much will it cost?" asked Mr. Tarky and passed the photo to Mary.

"Oooooooooh! Mr. Hedra! How did he go missing? What happened to him?" exclaimed Mary and stood up from her chair. She looked very shocked!

All our friends looked aghast in turn!

"What? How do you know Prof. Hedra?" asked Mr. Tarky.

"He is the science professor in my niece's school. He had joined recently, which of course, you must already know. I have met him. Such a good person! This is very sad. I will immediately...." Mary started speaking.

"Oh wait, no! Miss Mary, I don't think we need to take out any advertisements at the moment. Very silly of us, we never checked at the school office! Do not inform anyone as yet! Bye! Nice to see you," said Mr. Tarky and hurriedly snatched the photo back.

"But..." said Miss Mary.

Mr. Tarky signalled the kids to leave.

"By the way, which school does your nephew go to?" he asked while retreating.

"My niece. Surely you must already know that she goes to Rymond Academy. Same as your unc..." started Mary.

"Oh yes, of course. I was not thinking. Same as my uncle! We have to hurry now. Bye, Miss Mary. Thank you very much!"

All of them marched out of the office swiftly.

"Ha! Aren't we lucky! I was not expecting this!" said Bardek, in great excitement!

"Maybe Earth IS a magical place!" piped up Ruby from under Alisha's hat.

"Mr. Tarky, the schools are closed for holidays. How will we find Prof. Hedra? He may be away somewhere for a vacation!" exclaimed Alisha.

"Oh, Alisha! You should know that most teachers still go to school during the holidays. Prof. Hedra may still be here. Let's try to find him!" said Reyaan.

"Right! Now, where is this Rymond Academy?" said Mr. Tarky cheerfully.

Soon, everyone reached the school. But there was no way to get in as a big lock hung from the gates!

"Oh no! The school is closed! Now how will we get in?" Bardek looked dismayed.

"Let's climb over the gate," said Mr. Tarky.

"What is the point? There won't be anyone inside. And what if someone sees us?" asked

Reyaan uneasily.

"Fine, I will go in tonight. We may still find some clues about Prof. Hedra. Let's not waste any more time! If you want to join me, then do so. Else, I am going in alone!" declared Mr. Tarky.

"But I cannot come in the night!" wailed Bardek.

"Can you smuggle yourself out like we did the last time? The portal is right in your garden. We will also sneak out after dinner when everyone is asleep!" said Alisha.

Bardek thought that was a sound idea indeed and agreed to meet everyone else in the garden later in the night.

"Let's all get some rest now! We have a lot to accomplish tonight!" said Mr. Tarky.

However, when the gang reached the school later that night, another problem greeted them.

A guard was standing at the gate!

"Why is there a guard in the night? No one was here in the afternoon!" exclaimed Ruby.

"What are we to do? Now, we cannot climb over the gate!" wailed Bardek.

"Shhh… maybe we should climb over the walls from the other side instead," whispered Mr. Tarky.

"But the walls are so high! We will need a long ladder, and we don't have one!" said Reyaan.

"Let me think," said Mr. Tarky pacing around.

"There is no need to think. I can fly over the wall and get inside the school! Then I will look around to see if I can find anything," announced brave little Ruby.

"Err, well, that is one way. But I also wanted to…" began Mr. Tarky.

Bardek interrupted him, "that's wonderful Ruby! But what if someone catches you? You may have to live in a cage forever! We won't be there to save you!"

Ruby expanded herself to her full height, which

wasn't much!

"I am not afraid! I am going in now for the sake of Yoziland!" she proclaimed.

So, over the wall went little Ruby, her tiny arms flapping wildly!

She floated from door-to-door in the school corridors, but alas! All doors seemed to be shut tight! What was she to do!

On circling around the building, she spotted a light in one of the rooms on the second floor.

She flew to the window and peeped inside to investigate. No one was inside, and the window was closed.

A flummoxed Ruby wondered how to get in when she saw an air vent high up on the wall!

"Wait! I don't need doors or windows to get in. I am tiny!" said Ruby to herself.

She flew in through the air vent and entered the room.

Ruby hovered around the room to see if there

was anything useful when suddenly, she heard loud footsteps and voices. She immediately hid under the table.

Two people were talking.

"As I was saying, Prof. Hedra, we should consider setting up a science exhibition for the second term," she heard one of the voices say.

"Prof Hedra! I must catch him alone! What should I do?"

Now Ruby could have waited for an opportunity to attract his attention, but she was a bit impatient. Waiting was not for her!

She thought hard, and then she flew low over the floor and into the next room.

Neither of the professors noticed her as they were too engrossed in their discussion.

Ruby planned to make a loud noise to distract them, so she looked for something to tip over. One of them would certainly come over to investigate the noise. The professors would be separated. That would give her a chance to hide in Prof. Hedra's pocket.

"Aha! This looks like a bookshelf. Perfect! Let me try pushing this. I am quite strong!"

She leaned against the shelf with all her strength! But it wouldn't budge! Now that upset Ruby! So, she rammed herself against the bookshelf in an attempt to topple it with force.

"Owwwwwwwwoooooot!" she screamed in pain.

Oh no! We all know how shrill Ruby's voice is, don't we?

She quickly flew to the top of the shelf in panic!

Unfortunately, both the professors came running from the other room on hearing such an unusual noise.

Now, how will Ruby hide in Prof. Hedra's pocket?

The lights were switched on, but they couldn't find anything amiss. Poor Ruby had not been able to move the heavy shelf by even a millimetre!

"Oh, that must have been an owl outside. Although, it sounded like the shriek came from this room!" said the other professor.

"Prof. Wilson, I think we should go home now. It is very late. You go ahead, I will wrap up our work before leaving," Ruby heard Prof. Hedra say.

"Will you do that? Thanks! I will see you tomorrow then!" said Prof. Wilson and left.

"Wonderful! Perfect time to appear!" thought Ruby as she followed Prof. Hedra to the other room.

"Prof. Hedra! Hello!" she whispered in his ear.

"Yaaaaaargh! Who are you? Help!" shouted Prof. Hedra on spotting Ruby. He looked terrified, for a grown-up man!

"Don't be alarmed. I come from Yoziland. My name is Ruby and your friend Mr. Patra has sent me. I am here to help you!" said Ruby hurriedly in one breath!

"WHAT! Patra sent you? YESSSSSS! I can finally go home!" shouted Prof. Hedra in delight!

Ruby gave a quick account of who she was and why she was there. Prof. Hedra looked very, very relieved!

"Look, Ruby, I am stuck in this world! I cannot find the tree portal through which I came here. I have been trying several houses every night to get back home!" he said.

"But now, you can take me back! Let's go and meet your friends!" he continued.

He hid Ruby in his stack of files, and she led him to the spot where all the others were waiting.

"Prof. Hedra!" cried Mr. Tarky with joy.

"Well done, Ruby!" said everyone else!

Ruby was quite proud of herself! I do think that Alisha's hat got a bit small for Ruby on the way back home! So puffed up she was!

CHAPTER SEVEN

Everyone made their way to Prof. Hedra's house, where he made some tea for all. Then he told his tale of what he had been up to all these days!

"When I was a child, I found a tree portal in my backyard. I came to Earth through it many times and had many incredible adventures here!" he said.

"However, I soon understood that it was a dangerous thing to do, so I never told anyone else about it."

"Kids, you must know that the portal should be used only if there is an emergency! It is not to be played around with!" he warned.

"But why?" We use it all the time and we have been fine!" exclaimed Reyaan.

"What you don't know is that the portal travels every few decades. Once the original tree holding the portal dies, it chooses a new tree! The opening on the other side also changes location when this happens."

"The tree through which I travelled to this world last year, was unfortunately cut down by the owner, and I have been stuck here ever since!" said Prof. Hedra.

He continued his story and explained that he decided to obtain pure potassium while looking for the tree portal. He joined the science department in Rymond Academy and used the school lab to extract potassium during the nights.

"I took special permission from the school to work at the school lab in the nights. Mostly, I work alone, but Prof. Wilson joins me sometimes for his personal work, so I have to be very careful."

"I have already gathered enough potassium to start the process of cleaning Yoziland's atmosphere!" said Prof. Hedra.

"I thought that I would be stuck here forever! But now we can go home immediately!" he continued in rapture.

Oh, how pleased he looked!

"Great! So can we carry the potassium to Yoziland now?" asked a very curious Bardek.

"Not you dear, Bardek! Children should not be playing with chemicals!" exclaimed Prof. Hedra. "I will carry it. And yes, the sooner, the better! We will go home tomorrow. I cannot wait!"

"But you cannot leave just like that!" cried Alisha. "People will be looking for you!"

"I will leave a note for the school! Anyway, the holidays are on. I can get away for a few days." said Prof. Hedra.

"Ha! Do you know that we almost reported you as a 'Missing Person' today? Please do not disappear without covering your tracks!" said

Mr. Tarky.

"Don't worry! If we are successful in our mission, then I will come back to Earth for more potassium," assured the professor.

"Yay! We are all looking forward to seeing the blue skies in Yoziland again!" exclaimed Reyaan.

"Sorry kids. You haven't been listening to me. You cannot come to Yoziland anymore! I appreciate your help. But you must not travel through the portal again. I may still use it, but only because I have to!" said Prof. Hedra solemnly.

"But our apple tree will live for many more years! Nothing will happen to us!" cried Alisha.

"I think Prof. Hedra is right," interrupted Mr. Tarky. "We cannot risk your lives. Bardek, you mustn't travel to Earth again either. You must say your goodbyes to Alisha and Reyaan now!"

The children were crushed to hear that they would not see each other again!

It was decided that Prof. Hedra would reach

Reyaan's garden early in the morning and leave for Yoziland immediately with Mr. Tarky and Ruby.

And so, it was with heavy hearts that the kids parted. There was a lot of sniffing and sobbing as Bardek left for his home, but I will not describe the sad parts as much!

The following morning, the kids woke up to Mother's yelling. "Wake up, lazy heads! You should at least help me clean the house!"

"Uhh… what? Why? It is too early!" mumbled Alisha sleepily.

"Of course! But we have to start early. All our friends will be here for lunch soon! Don't you remember that there is a barbecue in the garden today?"

"Whaaat? What barbecue? You never told us anything!"

But mom was already out of the room, picking up stuff on the way.

"Father is in the garden. See if he needs any help!" her voice carried over from the other room.

Reyaan bolted upright immediately! "OH NO, Alisha! The HIDEOUT! Dad might find it! We must warn Mr. Tarky and Ruby NOW!" shouted Reyaan.

"And who will tell Prof. Hedra not to come here?" squealed Alisha.

"There is no time now — first we must stop Father from finding the hideout! You tackle mom. I will stall dad."

Reyaan raced out to the garden and found his father holding the gardening shears. "Dad!" he shouted. "What are you doing?"

"Oh, there you are. Reyaan, I will trim a few bushes and maybe some branches of this tree before the guests start coming in. I should have done this before, but I haven't been in the garden lately. Why does it look so messy suddenly?" said Father as he surveyed the garden.

"No, no you mustn't!" Reyaan grabbed the

shears from his father's hands. He was afraid that Father might cut off the magic apple tree branch!

"Isn't it too late to spruce up the garden now, dad? It looks fine anyway. Mother will be upset if the chairs are not ready and the umbrellas are not set up," he said, hoping to distract Father from the bushes.

"Please, can you help bring the furniture outside, dad? It is too heavy for me. I will clear the area in the meantime," he added pleadingly for good measure.

"Hmm, I suppose you are right. Let me get the chairs," said Father and headed inside.

Reyaan dashed to the hideout behind the bushes and found Mr. Tarky peeping through the leaves.

"Quick! Get out now and take all the stuff with you. Father will be here in a moment! There is a garden party here today. Try to stop Prof. Hedra at the gate."

Mr. Tarky disappeared with Ruby in a flash. Just in time! Father was already out with some of the garden furniture.

"Can you set these up?" he asked.

"Of course, dad!" said Reyaan.

"We will tell everyone…" Father began when suddenly he was cut off by a very loud noise.

This was followed by a shrill shriek from the front of the house. The shriek belonged to Mother!

"Oh no!" thought Reyaan. Had she seen Mr. Tarky in all his glorious wamlit form while he was escaping?

He rushed towards the gate along with Father. Alisha was already there.

What a sight!

Prof. Hedra was sprawled on the porch with a huge barrel by his side. Mother was standing right next to him, waving her hands. Thankfully, Mr. Tarky was nowhere to be seen.

"I had just washed the front porch when he suddenly popped up from nowhere and slipped on the soap suds," she gestured frantically at the figure stretched on the floor.

"Prof. Hedra, are you okay?" Alisha ran up to him.

"Ohhhh!" groaned Prof. Hedra as he slowly regained his senses. He proceeded to ignore everyone around him and immediately started inspecting the barrel that had rolled away from him!

The barrel looked enormous and very heavy! "Thank heavens! This is fine," muttered Prof. Hedra.

"Are you injured?" asked Alisha again.

"Do you know him?" a very puzzled Father asked, turning to Alisha. Mother still seemed to be recovering from her initial shock.

"Oh yes! Don't you know Prof. Hedra? He is the famous science professor from Rymond Academy!" exclaimed Reyaan in panic.

"Oh," said Father doubtfully. He wondered how his kids knew this professor from another school!

"To what do we owe the pleasure, Mr. Hedra? I hope that you are not hurt. Please do come in," said Father extending his hand.

"Errr… yes… no…I mean yes," stammered Prof. Hedra, who was a bit disoriented after the fall.

He was not very sure what to do. As per the kids, no one should have been stirring this early in the morning!

"Sorry to have bothered you like this. I am quite fine," said Prof. Hedra and grabbed his barrel tight. Clearly, its contents were very precious to him!

Now Father was almost as bewildered as Prof. Hedra.

I would be rattled too, dear children, if a stranger with a big barrel turns up at my house this early in the morning, and my kids claim to know him!

As they all went inside the house, Father was even more surprised when the professor rolled over his barrel right into the living room!

"What is in this tub?" he asked Prof. Hedra

politely. He tried his best not to look annoyed.

"Errr.. this is just oil," replied Prof. Hedra and fell silent.

Father looked expectantly at him, waiting for an explanation of this visit. They had guests coming over soon, and he hoped that this strange person would leave quickly.

"Well, you see, I came here this morning because… because…" started Prof. Hedra.

"I invited him!" said Reyaan, suddenly.

"You invited him? How did you meet him?" Mother asked, quite perplexed.

"We met him in the park a few days ago, where he was running a free science programme for kids. Mom, you know that we have such an interest in science. Prof. Hedra was kind enough to teach both of us some basic experiments the other day!"

"In the park?" asked Mother incredulously.

"Well, yes, yes, it was all very safe… very, very safe. Don't you worry! Reyaan and Alisha are very bright children. They insisted that I meet…" started Prof. Hedra uncomfortably.

But Father warmed up upon hearing that the children were putting their holidays to good use.

"Reyaan, it was very nice of you to invite the professor to meet us, although you should have informed us earlier!"

"Mr. Hedra, we are having a barbecue today. You must stay for lunch!" Father promptly asked Prof. Hedra.

"This is perfect!" thought Prof. Hedra. It was just a matter of a few hours, and it will be easier to escape back to Yoziland right after the party.

"Why, very kind of you, sir! I will stay for lunch!" he declared.

"This is lovely. But I don't understand why you brought this oil here. Can we keep this barrel outside, in the porch?" asked Mother.

"Err.. you see, I was planning to visit another friend after meeting you. He…err…he needs this oil for some err.. research. I cannot keep it out in the sunlight for very long as the light exposure can spoil it."

"Can I keep this safe, somewhere inside the house till I leave? I don't want your guests tripping on it," Prof. Hedra asked Mother.

"Of course! Here, let me keep this in the store for the time being," said Mother.

But Prof. Hedra immediately grabbed the barrel as if his life depended on it!

"Let me not bother you, madam. It is very heavy. If the children show me around to the store, I can keep it myself!"

So off he went with the kids to the store, rolling his barrel very carefully along the corridor.

"Is this potassium, Prof. Hedra?" whispered Alisha.

"Yes, dear, the pure metal is stored inside the barrel in lots of oil. We cannot keep it in the open as it can be risky! Now, children, you must promise me not to touch this barrel at all!"

"We promise!" chorused the kids.

"I will escape through the portal once the lunch is over."

Prof. Hedra looked elated. I am sure that Mr. Tarky and Ruby were not so elated though — stuck somewhere outside the house with nowhere to go!

CHAPTER EIGHT

S oon, the guests started pouring in!
The garden looked beautiful. The children had done a great job decorating it.

The food looked even better!
There were all kinds of delicious stuff to eat and drink.

Prof. Hedra ate till his shirt buttons threatened to pop out!

After all, he won't get to sample these earthly delights for a long time to come, will he?

After having his fill, he sat in a chair, sunning

himself and chatting idly with guests that walked by.

All looked good! He was feeling sleepy when he felt a faint buzzing in his ear.

"Wake up, Prof. Hedra!" someone whispered.

"Huh! Who is it? Ruby! Quick hide in my pocket! Someone will see you!" he said, looking furtively over his shoulder.

"What are you doing here?" he mumbled so that no one else could hear him.

"I came back!" said Ruby.

"I am so tiny that I can hide anywhere easily. I also wanted to try some of this delicious food," she continued.

"Anyway, I came to warn you that there are some naughty kids inside the house running amuck. I hope that you have hidden your potassium well!"

"Whaaaaaa! That's preposterous! I must check!" Prof. Hedra leapt up from his chair and dashed inside the house.

On the way, he stumbled over one football, two pillows, and several marbles!

"Ow..ow..ow!" he howled as he rushed straight to the store.

Reyaan and Alisha were nowhere to be seen, and the store door was open!

Prof. Hedra peeked in cautiously and almost fainted in shock when he saw a huge furry creature inside!

What was a furry creature doing here?

On closer inspection, he found that it was a dog. A dog who was sniffing his barrel with great interest. And it was a massive dog too!

"SHOO!" shouted Prof. Hedra and tried to shoo it away. But the dog wouldn't budge. Instead, it got very excited and started leaping in the air to lick his face. Prof. Hedra loved earthly-dogs, but now was not the time to befriend one.

"Oh no! How did it even get in here?" he muttered to himself in disbelief.

"Hello," someone whispered suddenly from behind the barrel. Prof. Hedra nearly jumped out of his skin in shock!

"How many of you are in here?" he hollered.

"Don't be so loud. We are playing hide-and-seek, and I am hiding here," said the voice. It belonged to a kid.

"You can't hide here! And where did this dog come from?" yelled Prof. Hedra as he tried to protect his barrel.

"This is my dog, 'Bean'. It follows me everywhere. Please don't be so loud," whispered the voice again.

"Can you please take it away?" pleaded Prof. Hedra, as Bean was now trying to wrestle him to the floor.

"FOUND YOU FRED!" said a squeaky voice behind him suddenly.

Fred didn't look too happy. "Oh NO! You were so loud that Priya found me! Come on Bean, let's go!" he said.

But Bean liked Prof. Hedra very much. He wouldn't stop jumping around, and Fred finally had to drag him away by the collar!

Prof. Hedra was left very shaken by this episode. Now, he was not too keen on leaving his precious barrel alone. After all, it held a lot of potassium, which was not safe for anyone and especially not the kids!

He looked around the house for Reyaan and Alisha and found them hiding behind the curtains.

"Quick, I must go home now! Show me that twig in the apple tree."

"Why? You cannot go now, Prof. Hedra! There are so many people in the garden!" squawked Reyaan in disbelief.

"Can't you leave in the night?" asked an equally baffled Alisha.

But Prof. Hedra wanted to rush home as soon as possible. So frightened was he, of little children!

"Kids, you have to help me! Get me out of here

NOW, for everyone's safety!" he implored.

Alisha thought quickly and said, "Reyaan, we need to get all the guests inside, else Prof. Hedra cannot execute his vanishing act."

"Yes, but we cannot do that. Who will listen to us?" said Reyaan.

"Can you play your piano for everyone? We can say that you want to showcase your amazing skill! Everyone will have to come inside the house to hear you," said Alisha.

But why was she grinning so wickedly when she said that? You see, Reyaan did not like playing the piano at all, even though he took classes every week. And he certainly did not enjoy playing in front of others!

"Certainly not, Alisha! What a silly idea!" he exclaimed.

"I say that it is a brilliant idea, Alisha!" said Prof. Hedra. "Can you play the piano, Reyaan?"

"Only if Alisha sings," said Reyaan glaring at Alisha.

Now it was Alisha's turn to glare back. "I DO NOT want to sing for anyone!"

"Why? We have to play long enough for Prof. Hedra to escape. You can sing after I play the piano," said Reyaan cheerfully.

"Great, you will play the piano and Alisha will sing. It will give me enough time to escape! Let's all go!" said Prof. Hedra.

"Wait, Prof. Hedra! I forgot to tell you where the magic branch is. Shake the lowest twig on the apple tree. It is the switch to the portal," said Reyaan.

"The lowest twig, you say? Oh, no wonder that you found the portal so easily. Usually, the switch is very well-hidden! But now is not the time to talk about it," exclaimed Prof. Hedra.

"Come, let's hurry!"

As soon as Reyaan opened his piano, the other kids crowded around him. All of them were very eager to perform as well!

Fred wanted to show off his Taekwondo moves, Priya wanted to recite her poems, and Toby wanted to be a mime!

My, my! What a talented lot!

Soon, a hastily-planned 'Talent-Show' was declared. All the parents were only too happy to see the wonderful performances, and so, everyone gathered inside the living room.

Even though it was very sudden, I think the show went very well indeed! I had no idea that Reyaan could play the piano so well and Alisha could hit the high notes!

Prof. Hedra decided to exit when Priya took the stage for her poetry.

"Mr. Singh, it was lovely to meet you…" he leaned towards Father and whispered.

"THERE ONCE WAS A NAUGHTY BOY CALLED BRYAN,
WHO THOUGHT HE WAS A LION."

Errr.. sorry, this was Priya. I was so mesmerised by her poems.

"Apologies, I have to leave for my friend's

house now, so I will just show myself out," continued Prof. Hedra.

"BUT IT WAS A TRUE FACT,
THAT HE WASN'T EVEN A CAT!"

"Please, I don't want you to miss the splendid performances. Don't bother getting up and do pass my thanks to Mrs. Singh."

Saying this, Prof. Hedra tip-toed out of the room and into the store.

He rolled his barrel away as discreetly as he could, out into the garden, and right under the apple tree.

"Great! I will be back in Yoziland in a few seconds. And no one has seen me!" thought Prof. Hedra as he disappeared into the portal with his prized load!

But Prof. Hedra, someone did see you! When everyone else was enjoying the show, Bean followed you to the garden! And then he sniffed around the tree looking for you when you evaporated right before his eyes!

What if he accidentally shakes the lowest twig in the apple tree?

POOOOOF!!

Oh no! Goodbye Bean! He found the magical twig and was sent off to Yoziland! I think it was his wagging tail that did it.

POOOOOOF!!!

Thank heavens! He managed to find his way back to Earth instantly. Good boy, Bean!

Hmm. But now, he does know something that only Reyaan and Alisha know.

♠

"Aah! The party went very well, I must say! Kids, you were marvellous!" declared a delighted Mother, after all the guests had left. "It's time to tidy up the place!"

Soon, the garden was cleared and the furniture was put away. Mother and Father were very tired, so they went inside the house for a quick nap.

Now it was time to say goodbye to Mr. Tarky and Ruby.

Poor Mr. Tarky had been hiding on a tree outside on the street all this while! Luckily, Reyaan had very kindly saved some food for him!

"I am losing two dedicated members of my team! That makes me very sad," said Mr. Tarky unhappily as he prepared to leave.

"Looks like all good things do come to an end. But maybe we will meet again someday!" said Ruby. She looked very miserable too.

"Don't look so glum, Ruby! We will send letters through Prof. Hedra when he returns to Earth, and you must do the same," said Alisha.

The children also had some sweet little souvenirs to cheer up Mr. Tarky and Ruby!
Reyaan gave Mr. Tarky his favourite multi-coloured pen, and Alisha gave Ruby her tiniest hair clip! It was still huge for her itty-bitty head!

And then, with one final shake to the magical apple tree twig, both disappeared!

Did it all go well in Yoziland?
Well, that is a story for another time, kids!
But I assure you that Mr. Tarky and Ruby went on to

have many more adventures and misadventures back home!

Toodles!

THE END

About Mr. Tarky

Did you know that Mr. Tarky used to work as a researcher before he became a refordest? He loves to play a lot of sports, but swimming is his favourite activity! In fact, he won the Salazia swimming championship when he was seventeen!

What do you think he looks like? You can draw Mr. Tarky in the space below.

About Ruby

Ruby is our brave adventurer! She is very curious and loves to explore the great outdoors. For a creature-in-hiding, she is very well-travelled indeed. Of course, it helps that she doesn't have to buy airplane tickets!

What do you think she looks like? You can draw Ruby in the space below.

About Bardek

Bardek reads a lot of books. He knows a lot about the different cultures and history of Yoziland. He wants to be a tourist guide when he grows up. I would say that he is off to a great start, as he has already travelled to planet Earth!

What do you think he looks like? You can draw Bardek in the space below.

ABOUT THE AUTHOR

Shivangi Nainwal grew up in Dehradun, India, where she built many a kingdom and foiled many a robbery – all in her imagination! After working in technology for several years, she has now decided to chase a few legendary dragons again. She currently resides in London, and 'The Untold Tales of Yoziland' is her first book.

Printed in Great Britain
by Amazon

79593111R00068